This 1987 edition published by Derrydale Books,
distributed by Crown Publishers,
Inc., 225 Park Avenue South, New York,
New York 10003.

ISBN 0-517-65492-X
h g f e d c b a

# THE BEST BEDTIME STORIES

## OF MOTHER MOUSE

A story by
Anne-Marie Dalmais
illustrated by
Violayne Hulné

English translation by
DIANE COHEN

**DERRYDALE BOOKS**
New York

When Mother Mouse walks into her little ones' room, there's a real racket going on! Young mice are scampering every which way. Their somersaults and acrobatics have turned their beds upside down! Pillows and covers are flying through the air. Toys are scattered, here and there, on the floor. Oh what a lively sight these nine mischievous little mice make! One is hiding in the toy chest, some are hopping and leaping, while the others are playfully dancing around in a circle, singing at the top of their lungs:

*First step to the right, then step to the left.*
*How we love to eat radishes and peas!*
*Now jump forward, now jump back.*
*Hooray for chocolate and Swiss cheese!*
*Tra-la-la, tra-la-la, hop, hop, hop!*

These little mice don't look the least bit sleepy!
And yet, it's almost time for bed.

What's a Mother Mouse to do? How is she going to calm her little trouble makers?

A magic wand would do the trick....

But you know very well mothers don't have them.

Nevertheless, Mother Mouse walks into the middle of this mess and muddle with a smile on her face. She sits down in a chair and says in her sweet voice:

"If you are quiet, my darlings, I'll tell you a story. And if you are *very* quiet, my little darlings, I'll tell you *two* stories!"

These words work like magic! All the little mice hurry to their mother's side, quiet down at once, and are all ears.

# The Attic Wardrobe

Once upon a time, there was a lovely little mouse whose name was Precious Pearl.

She had no brothers or sisters; this mouse was an only child.

She lived with her father and her mother in a comfortable little house, tucked away in the roots of a huge oak tree.

Precious Pearl had everything a mouse could want to play with: a pretty room, a beautiful doll, entertaining picture books, neatly sharpened crayons. But in spite of this, sometimes she was bored; for, what Precious Pearl loved more than anything else was conversation. Oh, how she loved to chitchat!

But when you have no brothers or sisters, it's not always easy... So our little mouse often felt quite lonely and sad especially on rainy afternoons like this one.

For the last fifteen minutes, Precious Pearl has been watching the raindrops trickle down her window pane. How she sighed. How she yawned. And she muttered: "Oh I don't know what to do...."

Just then, the squirrels, who lived on the top floor of the oak tree, came and invited her to play. There were three of them: Basil, Parsley, and Oregano.

Following them, the little mouse happily climbed the spiral staircase that led to their home.

"Since it's raining," Mother Squirrel said, "I'll let you play in the attic. Here's the key!"

The attic was nestled at the top of the tree.

"Gee! It's great to be up so high!" thought Precious Pearl.

She had never climbed to such heights!

She didn't feel the least bit dizzy.

Oh no!... just the opposite-she's amazed at how far she can see...

...then she opened the door and entered Wonderland.

She discovered a trunk full of antique clothes!

"What lovely shawls!" she exclaimed.

"What exquisite hats!" Oregano said with delight.

Meanwhile, her brothers were spining tops on the floor.

The little band was having a ball.

Precious Pearl was so happy!

Her black eyes sparkled while she chattered away to her heart's content.

Suddenly our friends heard footsteps on the stairs.

"It must be Mother!" Basil said. "Let's hide just for fun!"

"Where? Behind the trunk?" Oregano asked.

"No! In the wardrobe," Parsley decided.

The three squirrels and the little mouse hid in the back of the large wardrobe.

Parsley carelessly closed the door behind him....

The attic floor creaked.

The four friends held their breath.

Soon they heard Mother Squirrel's voice, muffled by the thick wardrobe door:

"Children, where are you?"

Not a sound came from the hideout.

"They must have left and gone into the garden in spite of the rain," decided Mother Squirrel. "Oh well, I'll go there too."

Meanwhile, back inside the wardrobe, our little rascals thought they had been hiding long enough.

Basil wanted to get out.

Alas, the door didn't open from the inside.

They were locked in!

And poor Mother Squirrel, she'd run all over the meadow looking for them and now she really started to worry.

Her children and their little guest were nowhere to be found!
"What has become of them?" Mother Squirrel worried anxiously.
"Perhaps they've gone back to Precious Pearl's."
Quickly she hurried to Mother Mouse's house and knocked.

"Are my little squirrels here?" she immediately asked.
"Oh no!" Mother Mouse said, very much surprised. "I thought they were with you...."
Then Mother Squirrel frantically confessed that she had lost the whole band! Luckily Mother Mouse remained calm and asked a very smart question: "Are you really sure they are not in the attic?"

15

So the two mothers decided to go back together to that fateful attic!

Even before they got upstairs they heard the children yelling, banging, and moving about. Their sweet, familiar voices came from the wardrobe. With one turn of the key, Mother Mouse freed the captives!

16

Hop! Hop! Hop! Mouse and squirrels leaped out of their prison! Boy, were they glad to be out of there! And they were relieved too! Especially Oregano, who was *so* afraid of the dark....

Parsley and Basil weren't too proud of themselves. They wanted to play a trick on their mother, but it backfired on them! Precious Pearl, however, was completely enchanted by this whole affair. "What an adventure! What a neat adventure!" she repeated, laughing out loud.

Everyone enjoyed a scrumptious snack prepared by Mother Squirrel. Then Precious Pearl went back home with her mother. That night she snuggled up under the comforter and closed her eyes at once, so she could remember that marvelous afternoon in the attic — its surprises, conversations, and that long journey in the back of the wardrobe....

# A New Year's Eve
# Surprise Party

Once upon a time there was a charming and whimsical family of mice. They were called the Tutti-Fruttis.

The father was a gardener who loved his job. He painstakingly tended a large orchard and gave each tree tender loving care. Indeed, Mr. Tutti-Frutti loved fruit so much that he named each of his children after one!

His three daughters were called Plum, Pear, and Apple, and the youngest, a baby boy, was named Apricot. Everyone in the family thought these were the most beautiful names in the world.

The entire Tutti-Frutti family was invited to a New Year's Eve party by their friends, the Thorn-Thistles.

The three little mice started getting ready for the party in the early afternoon. The countryside could be rather dull in wintertime, so you can imagine how excited they must have been about going to a party!

They put on their most beautiful dresses, made from the finest fabric. Their mother, a true artist, had embroidered them with plums, pears, and apples.

When it was time to go, the little mice bundled up in their capes and put on big hats with ribbons.

Father Mouse tucked Baby Apricot into his carriage. At last everyone was ready!

The Tutti-Frutti family started on their way, with Father and Mother in front pushing the baby carriage. The little sisters, Plum, Pear, and Apple trotted behind them, one after the other. They headed towards the woods, since the Thorn-Thistles lived just on the other side, at the edge of a large corn field.

The sun was slowly setting, but the walk didn't usually take more than half an hour. So our mice should have arrived well before nightfall. Suddenly the sky darkened with threatening clouds. A strong wind triggered a terrible snowstorm!

In a matter of seconds, everything turned white, and it was impossible to see anything! And what's more, it was bitterly cold. The travelers, huddled over in the blizzard, were blinded by snowflakes and overcome by icy gusts of wind.

Mr. Tutti-Frutti tripped over the root of a large tree, almost toppled over, and bumped into the trunk. This is how he accidently discovered a wooden door.

He knocked and knocked again, but no one answered. The wind howled so loudly.

Finally, the door opened slightly and old Mr. Rabbit cautiously peeked his head out. He looked quite flabbergasted.

"We're lost," Father Mouse explained. "Can we stay here a few minutes?"

"Why certainly! Why certainly!" replied old Mr. Rabbit. "Do come in! Do come in!" The next minute the Tutti-Fruttis were nice and cozy inside the Rabbit's burrow and were well protected from the storm.

And old Mrs. Rabbit, with kind eyes, made them feel right at home. The poor mice were *so* cold!

"Give me your coats and capes, I'm going to put them aside to dry."

"We don't want to be any trouble," Mother Mouse protested.

"Oh please, it's no trouble at all!" said Mrs. Rabbit, smiling. "I'm also going to make some hot chocolate. You need something to warm you up!"

"We'll only stay a few minutes. We just want to rest a bit," Father Mouse promised.

"Don't be silly, don't be silly," cried old Mr. Rabbit. (He always said things twice, to make sure others understood him.) "You won't leave here until the storm is over. You won't leave here...."

Just then he was interrupted by thumping noises. Someone was knocking at his door.

Cautiously, old Mr. Rabbit opened the door halfway: Guess who were standing there, on his doorstep, shivering and covered with snow? It's the hedgehogs, the Tutti-Fruttis' friends! What a coincidence! Mr. and Mrs. Thorn-Thistle, and their two sons, Pin and Needle, happily rushed into the warm, cozy room.

They recounted their adventure. "When we saw the first snowflakes, we decided to go looking for our guests, the mice, with a big lantern, but we, too, were stranded by this terrible blizzard."

"How lucky we are to all meet in this hospitable house," said Mother Mouse.

"Let's celebrate this fortunate occasion!" declared kind old Mrs. Rabbit. "We'll ring in the New Year together!" "Hurray! Hip, hip, hurray!" shouted Pin and Needle, the young hedgehogs.

"Bravo! Bravo! Bravo!" applauded Apple, Plum, and Pear, the mice sisters.

"Thank you...." the parents replied, smiling with delight.

It was wonderful idea. In the wink of an eye, they put together a real party! Apple, who had discovered some silk flowers, arranged a beautiful bouquet. Plum and Pear helped their mother set the table. Sweet Mrs. Rabbit brought in a delicious-smelling dish. Old Mr. Rabbit took his violin out of its case and started singing a happy tune:

> *Wake up, my little violin,*
> *Get up, my faithful fiddle,*
> *Wake up, let the party begin!*

What a marvelous time these mice, rabbits, and hedgehogs had! They ate heartily, laughed and joked, sung a thousand-and-one songs, waltzed and polkaed, until they decided it was time to go to bed.

"There is only one guest room," Mrs. Rabbit kindly apologized. "But I'm sure you can all sleep there."

"Naturally!" the guests exclaimed. "Don't worry your whiskers about it!

Indeed, they all fit very neatly and easily. The entire mouse family, with the exception of Baby Apricot, settled in the big bed. Mother and Father Hedgehog camped in the chest, comfortably filled with many pillows. Pin slept in a laundry basket and Needle crawled into the rocking chair.

There is nothing like cuddling up under a toasty comforter, where it's warm and safe and dry, while a storm is raging outside. Our friends couldn't have been more comfortable. And each one whispered, before falling asleep, "Oh what a magical evening it was... Just like in a fairytale!"

While their mother is telling them the second story, the little mice are climbing into their bed, a comfy basket covered with quilts and cushions.

Soon they are quieting down and begin to feel very drowsy. They lay their cute little heads on the fluffy pillows and drift off to sleep, imagining they're floating away on billowy clouds....

Their mother's voice, melodious and soothing, rocks them to sleep, a voice sweet as honey, vanilla ice cream, and chocolate mousse, spinning these wondrous tales about the snow... the New Year's Eve party... the Tutti-Fruttis and the Thorn-Thistles.

At last, one after the other, the little mice doze off, as if by magic....

Mother Mouse has finished her story. She gets up and very quietly, on her tippy toes, leaves her children's room....